Graphic design and illustrations: Zapp
Story adaptation: Robyn Bryant

© 1995 Tormont Publications Inc.
   338 Saint Antoine St. East
   Montreal, Canada H2Y 1A3
   Tel. (514) 954-1441
   Fax (514) 954-5086

ISBN 2-89429-847-1

Printed in China

PUSS 'N BOOTS

TORMONT

There once was an old miller who had three sons. When he died, he left everything in his will to them. Simon, the eldest son, inherited the flour mill, Bert got his donkey and Ned, the youngest, got a cat.

$\mathcal{S}$imon soon set to work grinding flour. Bert headed for town with his donkey.

"I'm going to find work hauling things," he said.

Ned, meanwhile, tried to think of a way to make a living. "And that silly Puss is worse than useless, for I shall have to feed him, as well as myself," he grumbled.

"Do not be so glum, Master," the cat said. "I have a plan that will make us both rich."

"What can you do? You're only a cat!" Ned said.

"Give me a fine hat, a pair of good boots, and a large sack," Puss said. "I shall take care of the rest."

"Why not," Ned said miserably. "Things couldn't get much worse."

When the cat was dressed to his satisfaction, he left Ned sitting in a field, and headed for the nearest stream. Then he crouched on the bank and used his swift paws to pull a dozen gleaming fish from the water.

$\mathcal{H}$is sack bulging with fish, Puss strutted to the castle and asked to see the king.

"What business does a cat have with the King?" asked the gatekeeper.

"I have a gift from the Marquis of Carabas," Puss said. He was allowed in at once, and bowed before the King, the Queen, and their daughter, Princess Cecile.

"The Marquis of Carabas sends his greetings, and would like you to have these fish from his estate, Your Highness," Puss said.

"Tell the Marquis we appreciate his kindness," said the King. But when Puss left, the King whispered, "Who is this Marquis?"

"I've never heard of him," the Queen replied.

13

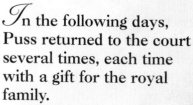

$\mathcal{I}$n the following days,
Puss returned to the court
several times, each time
with a gift for the royal
family.

"Here comes that
cat again! Who is this
Marquis of Carabas?"
the courtiers whispered.

Since no one knew the
answer, they made up things.
"I heard he is the richest man
in the kingdom," someone said.
"And the most handsome,"
said another.

One day, when Puss brought the Queen
a pheasant, she said, "Your Marquis seems
to be a good hunter."

"Oh yes, he has many talents,"
Puss replied.

"But why have we never met him?" the
Queen asked. "You must arrange a meeting!"

That night, Puss told Ned he was to
meet the Queen. "That's ridiculous!"
Ned said. "Look at me! I don't even own
a decent shirt!"

"Leave everything to me," Puss said.

The next day, Puss led Ned to the river. "Take off your shirt and get in the water," Puss told him.

"I can't swim," Ned said.

"Don't worry," Puss replied.

But when Ned stepped into the river, the cat pushed him into deep water. Just as Puss had planned, the current carried Ned downstream to the bridge where the King's carriage was passing.

"Help!" cried Ned.

"Hurry!" said Puss. "The Marquis is drowning!"

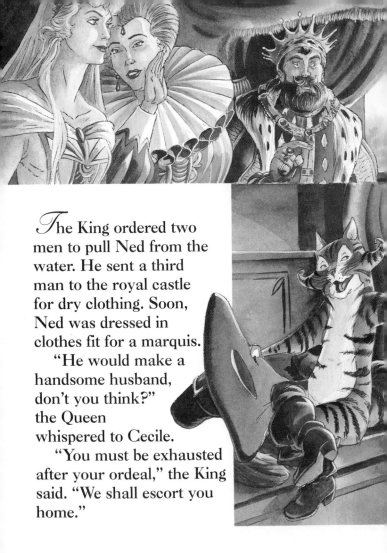

The King ordered two men to pull Ned from the water. He sent a third man to the royal castle for dry clothing. Soon, Ned was dressed in clothes fit for a marquis.

"He would make a handsome husband, don't you think?" the Queen whispered to Cecile.

"You must be exhausted after your ordeal," the King said. "We shall escort you home."

"*Y*es. Where exactly is your castle?" asked the King's advisor, who was suspicious of the cat and of Ned.

"Well, ahhh, I don't have a castle," Ned said.

"The Marquis is always so modest. There it is," said Puss, pointing to a castle on the hill. "Now, if you will excuse me, I have errands to run," Puss said, leaping from the carriage.

21

$\mathcal{P}$uss raced along the road ahead of the King's carriage, and shouted to the peasants working in the fields.

"If anyone asks, say these lands belong to the Marquis of Carabas," Puss told them. "The castle, too."

"Certainly, Sir," the peasants replied. Puss reached the castle on the hill, and knocked at the huge gate. A door in the gate swung silently open.

$\mathscr{P}$uss tiptoed through the dark rooms. Suddenly, a fierce ogre appeared. "What are you doing in my castle?" he shouted.

Puss introduced himself politely. "I hear you have magical powers, and can transform yourself into a lion or an elephant. Is that true?" Puss asked.

Instantly, the ogre transformed himself into a lion. "What do you think?" he roared, chasing Puss across the floor.

"I believe you!" said Puss. "But can you make yourself as small as a mouse?"

"*I* can do anything!" the ogre roared with pride. But as soon as he transformed himself into a mouse, Puss swooped him up and swallowed him in one gulp.

Meanwhile, the King's carriage was approaching. "Who owns all these rich fields?" the King asked.

"The Marquis of Carabas," a peasant replied.

"And the castle is his, too?" asked the King.

"Yes, Sire," said the peasant.

$\mathcal{P}$uss ran through the castle, opening
all the gloomy curtains to let the sun in.
He reached the gate just as the King's
carriage pulled up.

"Welcome to the castle of the
Marquis of Carabas," Puss announced,
bowing low.

"Why, it's lovely," said the Queen.

"*Y*ou've done very well for yourself,
young man," said the King.

"Yes, it seems that I have," replied Ned.
But in fact, Ned was not looking at the
castle. He had eyes only for Princess
Cecile. Several months later, the two were
married, and lived happily ever after. And
of course, Puss lived happily ever after
with them.